Save Me
That's small-town corruption
for you though, you can damn
near get away with fucking
murder when your daddy's the
only judge.

Save Me

Melissa C

Published by Melissa Current, 2024.

SAVE ME

First edition. August 2, 2024.

ISBN: 979-8227204189

Written by Melissa C.

I would like to take the time to thank my family for allowing me the freedom to spend my time writing. It has been a joy. I would also like to thank my readers. I hope I can continue to be inspired to create stories.

Chapter 1 Kaylee

My tears soak the pillow as they fall uncontrollably. The echo of his voice rings in my head, his words were cruel, I want to forget them, I always want to forget them. His grip on my neck was strong and unforgiving, and the force of his push had more intensity than times before. My back hurts from my landing on the hard coffee table, and my cries come out raspy as my throat struggles to recover. It all started off so small, a degrading comment here and there, slowly escalating to violence over the years. I made excuses for him for a long time. I would blame it on the liquor, but I deal with drunks all the time as a bar tender, and the liquor has nothing to do with it. Deep down, he's just a real piece of shit.

If he is home tomorrow, he will either act like nothing ever happened, or he will scold me for it being all my fault. He will make it seem like I will have deserved it. He will tell me how I did something to cross him, so I needed to be put in my place. He will go on and on about how his actions were somehow justified. He will then call his father to complain and that asshole will see it the same way. That's small-town corruption for you though, you can damn near get away with fucking murder when your daddy's the only judge. I sink my sore body further into my mattress and let the darkness consume me. In the morning it will just be a bad memory, until next time anyway.

I WOKE UP STIFF AND sore again, even after almost two days my throat still hurts like hell, so I decide to keep my breakfast strictly liquid again. The hot lemon tea offered a hint of relief as I swallowed down some aspirin. I blend up a blueberry banana smoothie to drink while I get ready for work. I feel a sense of relief when I see that Dewayne's truck is still gone, he took off the next day after making it clear that if I wasn't so lazy we would have more money, and I wouldn't have needed to be punished.

Aside from Dewayne being gone I am grateful that I paid the rent and stashed some money at the bar after I cashed my check because he has probably taken the rest. I check my purse only to find that I was right, that bastard took my fucking money. I hope this means the next few days will continue to be quiet because he'll be out drinking the money away. When he returns, he will probably try to act sweet for a while and then the cycle will start all over again. I'd like to say I could do something to avoid it happening again, but I know better.

I pick out a pair of dark blue jeans, a black tank top and flannel shirt. I am still not feeling like putting in much effort today but make up would help cover the bruising that has now formed on my neck. I put on my makeup, curl my long brunette hair and put it in a low ponytail on each side of my head to help hide any marks that might show through. At least it doesn't look like I'm trying to hide anything. I hate the questions, and I don't like having to make excuses for him. The less people that know the better, when people try to go up against the judge's son it never ends well for them... or me.

"GOOD AFTERNOON, KAYLEE" Jason says with his intoxicating smile as I walk through the doors of JP's Tavern for my shift. It's hard to be in a bad mood when you're greeted by that. I offer a smile and a wave in return as I walk behind the counter.

"Hi Kaylee, how was your weekend?" Maddox asks as he comes out of the supply room with a box of liquor bottles to stock.

"Uh, good." I say in a still raspy voice that catches everyone's attention. I can see Jason's reaction out of the corner of my eye. He knows, he always knows, it's hard to hide that shit form someone who's known you your whole life. I can see the anger flash in his eyes, and I know he can see the desperation in mine. There is no avoiding any damn questions now.

"Wow, sounds like you're coming down with a case of laryngitis." Jason says offering up some sort of a reason for me to sound like I do.

"Ya, that must be what it is. It was kind of sudden" I respond forcing the words.

"That's rough." Maddox says "Hey, do want me to cover your section tonight and you can mix drinks for me? It would be less talking" He offers. I smile and shake my head yes grateful that he bought it and didn't read much into the look that was plastered all over Jason's face.

"Thanks Maddox" Jason says as he keeps his eyes locked on me and motions for me to head to the back.

"Thanks" I whisper out to Jason trying to save my voice. He wasn't stupid, he knew this was Dewayne's handy work. He knew and he covered for me again just like always.

"Wanna talk about it?" He asks, the anger is still in his eyes, but he keeps his tone soft and full of concern. I simply shake my head no and start putting my stuff in my locker. I can't tell him right now, I can't let him know how scared I was this time.

"Alright. When you're ready then." he says softly as he turns to leave.

So far, he's the only one close to me who knows, it was just too hard to hide from him. He's my best friend, he also seems to have a pretty major big brother complex, so it really didn't take him long to figure it out. We grew up two houses apart, and at first, I was just Zane's annoying twin sister with cooties, but as we got older, they didn't mind me being around so much. By high school the three of us were thick as thieves. After Zane went off to college Jason seemed to get more protective, hence the big brother complex. He never liked Dewayne, from the moment he met him, and he never made any effort to hide it. If I hadn't been so fucking stubborn and blinded by lust back then, I would have taken Jason's advice and stayed plum away from Dewayne Lavey.

Chapter 2 Jason

The ringing of the alarm clock pulls me from my sleep, the bed groans as I roll over and debate hitting the snooze button. I've got deliveries coming in at noon, so I decided against the snooze and opted for coffee instead. The wood floor is cool on my bare feet, so I grab my slippers out of the closet, I'll be glad when the warmer weather gets here. As I make my way to the kitchen of my tiny one-bedroom bachelor pad, I can't help but think how nice it will be when all the renovations are done out at the bar. The apartment above it is huge, it was the thing that really drew me to that building when I was looking for a place to buy, and I am so ready for it to be done.

I had wanted to own a bar ever since I was a kid, I started saving when I was in high school. I put my time and focus on working and saving money instead of partying and dating. Zane always said I was missing out, but Kaylee and my parents said I was being smart. I was so excited when I finally had enough money saved to make my dream into a reality. I found the building and knew it would be perfect. There it was, an old, abandoned warehouse, it was pretty run down but there was just so much potential. The open floor plan gave me the freedom to design the layout perfectly; it was large enough to have a small kitchen to serve basic items like fries and burgers but nothing fancy. I was able to put in a pool hall as well as a small stage and a dance floor perfect for karaoke or a live band.

The apartment was the big selling point though, it is massive, with 3 bedrooms and 2 huge bathrooms. The living room and kitchen are open and spacious; it will make the ultimate bachelor pad but will transition well if I were to ever settle down. Eventually, I won't have far to go for work, and I will always be on site in case of a problem. I wish it wasn't taking so long to finish it though, it seems like one snag after another every time I turn around. Getting the bar up and going was the most important thing though, I can at least be making money while I wait, and this small place isn't too bad.

I hit the start button on the coffee pot and head to the bathroom to take a shower. I turn the water on as hot as it will go, the hot water helps ease the tension in my muscles. It's not even the stress of the bar and renovation hiccups that have me so tense lately, it's that fucking asshole Dewayne. He's been a dick ever since I have known him, he's always treating Kaylee like shit, like she is below him or some shit. He gradually escalated over time until one day a couple years ago he fucking hit her, she tried to hide it from me, but I knew. I wanted to kill him. The prick got away with it too, the cops never even took her statement that time, that's fucking small town corruption for you. One fucking judge in town and Dewayne's his only son. How's that for fucking luck.

Kaylee did think her luck changed once though, he had beat her pretty badly one night trying to in his words, teach her to be quiet. This time it wasn't Kaylee that called, it was an anonymous neighbor, the two cops who responded that night finally arrested him, the proof he beat her was all over her face.

That kind of fucking corruption runs deep though, he was out the next day, everything thrown out and covered up. The two officers who finally had the balls to arrest the low life got fucking fired for excessive force and harassing a young couple over a noise complaint call. I think Kaylee lost hope at that point.

That was the last time Dewayne ever hit her in the face though, his dad made it clear it was too hard to cover up that way. So there has been plenty of broken wrists and ankles since then, even some broken ribs, but no more black eyes. Now it seems he has escalated to chocking her out, she hid the bruises on her neck pretty well, but she sounded like her voice box was shattered. Just thinking about his hands on her makes my blood boil and my skin crawl. I have known Kaylee practically my whole life, she seems to have made it clear she thinks I only see her as a little sister, but she's more than that to me, she's my best friend. She's beautiful, smart, and she has a heart of gold, she deserves so much better, I can't help but be protective of her. I have managed to get Dewayne banned from the bar, I only got that lucky because it's in a different county, so the trespass held up, but I feel helpless aside from that. Dewayne is untouchable in Hamilton County with his dad sitting in the judge's seat, everyone who tries to take him down loses, and Kaylee gets beat, there is no happy ending. I'm afraid at this point her only way out is going to be when he kills her.

I drink a cup of coffee and grab a clean pair of blue jeans out of the dryer to go with my black t-shirt with the bar logo on it. I better head over to the tavern to accept the deliveries. I have 2 different liquor deliveries, a food truck coming, as well as flooring and counters coming for the apartment. The winter storms last week really delayed some of my shipments so now I am in for a really busy day.

Chapter 3 Kaylee

It's been a quiet couple of weeks and for that I am grateful. Dewayne has been in his sweet phase, his touch makes me want to vomit at this point, but I would rather have the sweet side of him, I don't really fancy being used as a punching bag. He took me grocery shopping yesterday, and today he is making me dinner. I have tried to be on my best behavior and cater to his every need, the longer he stays in this phase the better. It's safer for me, it is also nice to see the small glimpses of the man that he pretended to be all those years ago, back when I thought he was the only man for me.

I remember the night we met; Jason and I had gone out with a group of friends to celebrate an engagement. We were all drinking and throwing darts when I noticed Dewayne across the bar. He was so handsome, his dusty blond hair and broad shoulders had me practically drooling. I was drawn in and stuck on those piercing green eyes of his, his gaze was so intoxicating. I often think about how my life would be now if he had not caught me staring at him. He smiled at me when he noticed, and it made a blush creep up into my cheeks that I am sure he could see from across the room.

He thought he had so much game sending me over drinks, I fell for it though, I eventually walked over to him so I could thank him for the drinks. He flirted and swooned me right into his bed that night. It was amazing too, the way he scooped me up and pinned me against the wall so I could feel every bit of him grinding against me had me so turned on and hooked on him. Everything was so passionate at first. Jason told me to stay away, he said he knew that Dewayne was bad news. I refused to listen and instead, I insisted, rather rudely as I recall, that he was just trying to be an overprotective big brother because Zane moved and wasn't there to hover over me anymore. I am way too fucking stubborn for my own good sometimes. Jason could tell there was something off about him from the very start, but me, all I saw was a ridiculously good-looking man flirting with me.

After several months of flowers, surprise dates and steamy sex, I was so smitten with Dewayne that when he asked me to move in with him, I was more than happy to accept the offer. This is the point of our story that I wish I could rewrite. Once I moved in with him something dark started surfacing and it was ugly. It started as just snide comments in public, mostly around his friends. He would criticize my cooking, then laugh it off and tell me later he was joking. It all kind of escalated from there. He started making fun of me for "letting myself go" even though nothing had changed, I did my make up the same way, my hair was the same and I hadn't gained any weight. The dynamic in bed started to change as well, the passion slowly faded and was replaced by force and darker tastes. His friends all treated their wives and girlfriends the same way though. Those things were just the first of many red flags I ignored over time.

"Dinners ready Kaylee" Dewayne's words pull me from my thoughts

"It looks delicious honey, thank you." I replied with as big of a smile as I could muster up.

"Anything for my girl" his response makes me cringe a little as I take my first bite.

"'This deer steak is really great honey, thank you again" I say as I continue eating. The food really was good, Dewayne has so many faults, but he can cook. His talent is mostly grilled meat and fried potatoes paired with a cold beer, but I guess that's a pretty standard meal for small town USA. We never miss a hunting season of any kind out here, and we love our meat paired with potatoes and beer.

"Do you want more?" Dewayne asked me as he got up from the table

"No thank you, I'm trying to lose a few more pounds" I tell him, hoping to save myself from a few harsh words by pleasing him a little with my statement. The look on his face tells me I made the right call.

"That's my girl, can't have you getting any fatter now can I. Ok, well put this all away for my lunches and clean up, I'm meeting Jake and Mike at the bar." He says as he leaves. A wave of relief rushes over me as I realize I am safe for another night. I clean up the mess from dinner and I am sure to not leave anything out of place. I decide to tidy up the rest of the house before I take a shower.

The hot water relaxes me as I let it fall and consume me; the steam fills the shower like a dense fog. The calmness that it brings me is welcomed and all I want to do is stand here and enjoy it forever, it's my escape. My mental trip to paradise comes to an end as I start to lose the hot water. I step out of the shower and hug myself with my towel. I have no clue what tomorrow will bring but for now I will enjoy a safe night in my bed.

Chapter 4 Kaylee

"I need 3 Vodka cranberries please" I tell Jason with a smile as I set my tray down on the counter

"Coming right up" he says as he winks at me making me chuckle.

"So" He starts again "things have been good for a bit I've noticed" he says fishing for information. I haven't really talk it out with him yet like I usually do, so I knew this would be coming at some point.

"For now." I say as I shake my head and break eye contact. I know I need to talk to him; he is the only one who understands but this last time scared me, I am also ashamed that he always has to cover for me.

"Please talk to me tonight, I have been really worried about you. And I can tell you are avoiding something" he says as he puts my drinks up on the counter

"Ok" I whisper as I load my tray up with the drinks. He offers me one of his classic intoxicating smiles and I can't help but smile back at him. Best friend or not he really is quite handsome, a pain in my ass, but handsome.

It is Friday night, and this place is packed. Jason got a local band to play every Friday, so it really brings in a crowd. It makes for a really busy night, but it is great tips. It's also a great and welcomed distraction. I get to escape a little from the worry that comes with the uncertainties of home. I continue about my night running drinks and cleaning tables until I finally hear the bell for last call, I will finally be able to slow down a little. After the last customers leave Maddox locks up the main entrance, then the cleanup begins. We Have a pretty good routine down though so we can usually all get out of there in about an hour or so.

After the last of the crew left, I walked to my locker to grab my things and put my tips up. I keep my tips and whatever money I need out of my pay checks for bills stashed here in my locker and some in the safe in the office with Jason. Dewayne can't get to it that way so I can make sure the bills get paid. It also gives me a way to save some money that he doesn't know about just in case I can ever figure out how to leave him.

"Hey you, everyone's gone, we can head out now." I tell Jason as I get to the office door.

"I would like it if we could talk first Kaylee. It's been a couple of weeks now and you haven't...." He stops himself as he starts to show his frustration "I just really need to know you are ok." He adds after he softens his tone. I hesitate because I really don't want to relive it right now.

"This time I." I stop because my voice starts to crack, and I know I can't hold in the emotions. "I...I thought I was going to die Jason" I said as tears prick at my eyes and then start to fall like a warm rain.

"Ok, ok I got you" he said as he walked over and took me in his arms. He was exactly what I needed.

"You always...I am just so...." I can't even say everything I want to say through the tears and the emotion. I just cried there on his shoulder.

"I'm here, I'm always here" he said as he just held me and let me soak his shirt with my tears.

"You always cover for me" I finally say full of shame. I can't believe that I let my life come to this.

"I always will Kaylee, always." He says as his arms wrap tighter around me and instead of fear I feel comfort. His touch was soft, it was different this time, like maybe he looked at me differently than I thought he did, like maybe it was never a big brother complex at all, maybe it was more than that. I'm probably just over thinking it.

"I couldn't breathe!" I cried. "I couldn't breathe!" my chest felt tight and heavy as I relived that memory.

"You're alive, I'll get you out, I promise. I'll figure it out" He whispered as I sobbed in his arms. I didn't believe that he could, but I knew he would do everything he could to follow through.

He held me as I cried for what seemed like hours, it was what I needed, he made me feel safe. In that moment I didn't have to worry. I finally composed myself, caught my breath and wiped my tears. I grabbed my things, and he walked me to my car in silence. I knew as soon as I left the bar that I would be at the mercy of Dewayne's temper, my safety would be gone. I prayed that it would all work out before something worse happened. I trust Jason to try, but I am not sure if he can save me from this.

Chapter 5 Jason

I drove home with my heart clenched in my chest. I Would love nothing more than to get rid of that fucking prick Dewayne forever. I have got to figure out how to help get Kaylee out of there. I know she is scared to leave but there has got to be a way. He's going to end up killing her if she stays, he damn near killed her this time. I am haunted by her words "I couldn't breathe", her voice was full of fear, and it broke me, I can't lose her. She is scared and alone, I have got to do something.

Heavy thoughts plague my mind as I try to sleep. The bed groans as I toss and turn. Her words play over and over in my head. It's my fucking fault, I told her he was bad news, but I should have pushed it more. All she saw was Dewayne flirting and buying her drinks, but I knew there was something more sinister behind him. I had heard a few stories about him and the way he carried himself just rubbed me the wrong way. I didn't know he would end up beating her, but I never should have let Kaylee leave with him that night. After that night it was so easy for him to swoop in and manipulate her. The gifts came flowing in, the bouquets of flowers started showing up, she was hooked and there was no getting through to her.

He hid his inner monster from her well in the beginning I'll give him that. After she moved in with him, he knew he had full advantage of her. Kaylee had no clue how trapped she was going to be. He was able to gain control of her so fast and at first, she was completely oblivious to it. She always had so many excuses for him; it wasn't until he got really mean that she started to open up to me about how hard it was getting to be with him. She still tried to hide it from me when he hit her the first time. It was just a slap to the face, but it shook her. It only got worse from there. Watching him walk for beating her though really fucked with her, she realized then that she's, his prisoner.

I can't let this go on. I have to do something; the tension and the sleepless nights are killing me. All my time is spent worrying about Kaylee and trying to come up with ways to make Dewayne Lavey disappear. If I'm being entirely honest though it is probably regret that plagues me more than anything right now. My feelings for Kaylee had grown from best friends into more of a crush. I just didn't know how to make her see that when she couldn't even hardly seem to buy into the fact that I was not trying to act like her big brother. I was full of jealousy when Dewayne sent over that first drink, but when she saw my warnings and reservations as more of an overprotective big brother, I backed down too much. Looking back, I maybe should have told her how I feel.

Worry and regret continue to consume me, so I try to focus on happier thoughts, work even, in hopes of being able to drift off to sleep. It seems to work as I think back to when we all graduated. I had picked up an extra shift at the diner to help my mom out, it was hard managing it by herself, and I really wanted the extra money. I ended up missing the graduation party, but Kaylee made her friends ditch out on it early and come eat at the diner. She also made them leave a big tip so I could put it in my savings. She told them all that one day I was going to have the best bar in the valley. She has always supported me in everything I did.

The good memories of happier times calm my head, and I feel my eye lids finally getting heavy. Stillness takes over my body as I drift off to sleep. I welcome my slumber after the heaviness of the night, it will be another busy day tomorrow, full of deliveries and I need the rest.

Chapter 6 Kaylee

His large hand wraps around my wrist and gives an unforgiving pull. I cry out in pain as I feel myself being pulled from my bed and across the bedroom. Not fully awake and oriented yet, I struggle to stay on my feet, so I fall to the floor as I am dragged to the hallway.

"I'm sorry, Dewayne! I'm sorry" I cry. I apologize out of habit because at this point, I am not sure what I am in trouble for.

"Shut up you bitch!" He yells as he makes his way to the top of the stairs. With one quick motion he moves his grip from my wrist to my hair and starts down the stairs.

"Please, I'm sorry. Please stop." I cry as my body flops like a rag doll against the stairs.

"Fucking stupid worthless bitch! You think you can just leave dirty laundry in the hamper and not have dinner on the table. Your job is to wash the clothes, clean the house and make my food! Fucking no good whore, can't even do that." He screams but his words are slurred. I can tell he is completely wasted, but I can see the monster showing through in his eyes.

"It was late, I-I'm sorry, you were out with the guys, I didn't know you would be hungry in the middle of the night. I didn't mean to make you mad, h-honest. It's just one load of laundry;

I'll start it if you want" I barely finish getting the words out when I feel his large fist make contact with my cheek.

"Shut your fucking smart-ass mouth up! I didn't say you could fucking talk! You're a slob and a waste of space." He screams at me. I feel the blood start running from my nose and it mixes with the tears falling from my eyes. All I can do is cry and brace for what's coming. I scream out for help, but I know no one is coming, they never do. It has been almost 4 months since the last time; I don't normally get that long of a break anymore. His violence is escalated and sloppy, it will make the abuse harder for him to explain away. Clearly the violent monster he hides inside is taking hold, I am not sure I will survive this time, not this escalation.

"I just don't know why you can't behave right! Do what I tell you and only speak when I say you can. It's not that hard!" He screams in my face as gets on top of me. Blows to my face come one after another.

"Maybe it's time I shut you up for good!" He tells me as I feel the all too familiar grip around my neck, fear consumes me, and I am sure this is the end for me. His grip is firm and crushing, I feel myself unable to breathe.

"P-l-e" I try to beg for my life, but I can't get the words out. I feel myself start to fade and the world around me starts to go dark as I lay on my cold floor dying. I hear the front door slam, but the sound is faint and muffled, I want to move and call for help, but I can't. I am going to die here, alone, at the hands of the devil I couldn't escape. I feel my body getting colder as my consciousness slips away and darkness completely consumes me.

I HEAR FAINT BEEPING and muffled voices in the distance; the bright lights are blinding as I try to open my eyes. I don't know where I am, heaven maybe.

"Doctor! I think she is waking up" I hear a female voice saying, I guess I'm at a hospital or maybe I'm dreaming.

"Kaylee, can you hear me?" A man's voice questions. I try to speak but I can't. I do manage to open my eyes a little bit.

"Should I get her friend Dr. Stevens?" The female voice asks. Fear creeps in and my heart begins to race. What friend is she talking about, please not him. Please not Dewayne.

"Yes." the doctor says. "Kaylee, its ok. You are in the hospital, do you remember what happened?" He asks. I do remember and I am panicking they are bringing him right back to me.

"Kaylee." I hear a familiar voice but instead of more fear it calms me. "Kaylee, can you hear me, I'm here" he says. It's Jason, thank God he's here. I start to relax a little with his presence.

"Kaylee, I'm Dr. Stevens, it's nice to see you awake. Do you remember what happened?" He asks me. I can barely do it, but I shake my head yes slightly. Tears fill my eyes as I try not to relive the moment. I feel Jason take my hand and I try my best to clench it and not let go.

"You're safe here" Jason tells me, his voice is soft, and the touch of his hand is calming.

"Kaylee, you sustained trauma to your face which resulted in a surgery to repair, you have a few broken ribs, and you sustained some other fractures. There was also some minor damage done to your vocal cords. It will take some time to recover but with some rest and physical therapy you should be able to go home in not too long. I want to make sure you can talk, eat, and move around a little better. I'm glad your awake and I will be back later to check on you." Dr. Stevens says with a kind and soft tone. That was a lot of information to process, I am still groggy but very much aware of the pain that I am in.

"Hi Kaylee, I'm Rachel, I'll be your nurse today. I'm glad you're up, if you need anything let me know. I'll give you two sometime." She says in a very cheery voice. She seems nice and I want to smile at her, but I can't make my face do it.

"Thank you" Jason tells her as she leaves. He lets my hand go but only long enough to grab a chair to sit right next to the bed. He kisses my hand and hangs his head. I can see the tears forming in his eyes as he looks up to tell me he's sorry. I want to tell him it's not his fault, I want reach for him, but I can't, I am weak and my face hurts too bad to talk. My wounds start to sting as tears fall from my eyes.

"I will never let him touch you again! I thought I lost you!" he whispered. There was a part of me that was happy to be alive but there was also part of me that would rather be dead. I am in so much pain right now and as long as Dewayne is out there, I don't know that I will ever really be safe. I sure as hell don't believe I will get any justice.

Chapter 7 Jason

"Hey Maddox, I have a little bit of good news. Kaylee's awake, she has been for a few hours now. She's not out of the woods yet but it's an improvement." I tell Maddox over the phone; I have been waiting anxiously to make this call and give a good update.

"That is great news, I will be sure to make the announcement to the crew when things slow down. Everyone is coming together to cover the shifts. We really had no idea that she was going through all that man we're sorry." Maddox says, his voice full of sympathy. I know Kaylee is going to be upset and embarrassed when she realizes everyone knows now, but they needed too.

"She wanted it that way man, it's ok. I was just checking in, seeing how it's going and to give the good news." I tell him

"We're good, the apartments pretty much good to go now man. The furniture was delivered this morning, so you have a place to sit and a place to sleep." He tells me

"Thanks Maddox, you're the best manager I've had." I tell him with a chuckle

"You've got jokes." He laughs "I'm the only manager you've ever had, and I may need a raise after this" He jokes back, and I offer a laugh.

"Let me know if you have and trouble, Harrison County said they would try to up the patrol if we need it." I tell him. I may need to actually consider that raise for him, he really has stepped it up.

"Alright, no problem. Take care of your girl man" he tells me before hanging up.

I am so glad she is awake; I really thought I had lost her this time. Her recovery is going to be brutal and the trauma she had to endure is going to scar her for life. She is so beat up and it kills me. He crushed the bones in her face and broke her ribs. I hope that fucker gets brought to justice this time. If it wasn't for her neighbors, I don't know what would have happened. I'm glad they told the paramedics to bring her here.

"Ja-Ja" I hear Kaylee start to try to whisper as I step back into the hospital room

"Hey, I'm here. Take it easy." I tell her as I take her hand and rub soothing circles with my thumb

"Wh-Where" She struggles to get the words out, so I interject.

"Where are you?" I ask, hoping I guessed right. She nodded her head yes

"You're at Harrison Regional. You're safe" I reassure her, and it seems to help

"Ok" she whispers "I-I'm scared" she adds quietly

"I know. But he can't get you here, and my apartment is mostly ready so when we leave here, I'm taking you there. Get some rest now." I tell her in hopes to ease her mind a little bit so she can rest. She nods in response and closes her eyes.

It's true he can't come here, the cops took statements from me and the neighbor, they got their pictures, and they are hanging pretty close until they talk to Kaylee. The bad news is it happened at their house, in Hamilton County where he's protected by the fucking judge and everyone that piece of shit pays off. The cops over here are working really hard to bring up charges and make them stick but making a case from here will be difficult. As long as Dewayne's not locked behind bars, I don't think Kaylee will ever feel safe.

I get the chair made out into a bed; this is the same place I have slept for the last 3 nights. We have a lot to talk about, and I know she will have a lot of questions. So, we will both need the rest. Not only was it time to tell the crew down at the tavern but it was time to tell her family. Zane is pissed and I feel like I should give her a little warning before he gets back to town. Truth be told I'm a little scared of him, I let him down.

I didn't protect her, and I couldn't save her from this, all I can do is plead my case, maybe tell him how I feel about her, hopefully he will understand. I'll never let her out of my sight again, I'll do whatever it takes to take care of her now. There's no room to fuck this up, Dewayne almost killed her. I give Kaylee a kiss on her forehead and get settled down. I hope she feels better tomorrow.

Chapter 8 Kaylee

The parade of nurses and hospital staff in and out of my room wakes me. I am kind of happy to see them though, my body is starting to scream at me so I know I could use another dose of pain meds. My mouth is dry but so far all I get is liquid food pushed through the tube dangling from my nose, hopefully that changes soon, I could really go for some water right now. I could also use another shower, like a real one, alone, I feel so gross. I have been informed that I have to be able to walk better first before I get much privacy in that department. Jason and the doctor discussed that the physical therapy team would be in again today, so hopefully soon.

Jason hasn't left my side for days now, the furthest I have seen him go is just outside the door to make a call or go to the nurse's station. He has been living out of a backpack this whole time. He has also been more affectionate lately. He holds my hand and kisses my forehead, it feels nice, but I don't really know how to take it. He makes me feel safe so for now I will go with the flow and not question it, I know he thinks this is his fault.

"Good morning, Kaylee. How are you feeling today?" Dr. Stevens asks as he enters my room.

"Sore." I answer with a strained voice.

"I bet you are, but I am happy with your progress. So today I would like to start working towards walking and using a straw.

Nothing too crazy, it's going to be a few days before you are in good enough shape to go home, so we'll take it slow." He says in his normal soft tone.

"OK, thank you" I respond. He is kind and encouraging every time he speaks to me but the words "go home" make me feel a little empty, I can't go home. I do my best to offer a smile, I don't want to think about that right now.

"I'll be back later to check on you." He says as he leaves

"Thank you doctor" Jason tells him.

I know I have a long recovery ahead, and I have a packed day from the sounds of it, but I am anxious to talk to Jason more, he fills me in little by little about the case they are trying to build, but there is more I need to know. I am still confused; how did I get here? No one ever comes to help anymore. My screams have gone ignored for a couple years now. I am also worried about my family, I don't know if they know I'm even here. I never told them what was going on, I was too scared and embarrassed too. If Jason's here I'm sure that means that the crew at work knows, this feeling of shame really fucking sucks.

"Um, Kaylee, we uh probably need to talk about a few things today, other than the case I mean." Jason starts nervously "Please don't get mad at me, because I'm really sorry, but I had to tell people." He confesses to me answering some of the questions I had.

"I know you did" I say as I hang my head with shame. I knew I put him in a bad spot making him keep my secret.

"I'm really sorry, I know I promised, but you almost died." He says, seemingly still nervous as he sits on the edge of my bed.

"Jason, I'm not mad. It's ok." I say as I rest my hand on top of his trying to put him at ease. "I'm just embarrassed and ashamed.

I never should have asked you to keep this, and I should have listened to you" I add as tears threaten to prick my eyes.

"You don't need to be ashamed; everybody just wants you to be safe. Your parents are going to come by today. Your mom really wants to see you." He says as he takes my hand.

All I can do is nod as I wipe the tears from my face that are starting to fall. Worry takes it's hold as I wonder what they will think when they see me. I don't want them to be disappointed with me. I picked the wrong man; I hid the abuse and got stuck in a spot I never should have been in to begin with.

"What do I say to them" I ask him through worry

"Just that you love them, that's all they want to hear" Jason tells me as he extends a warm smile my way.

IT WAS A VERY LONG and emotional day, but it was good to get it all out and in the open. I had a good visit with my parents and Jason was right, all they wanted was for me to be safe. Zane will get into town tomorrow and will probably storm in here trying to be the tough guy, I just hope he will keep it together and not do anything stupid. I am glad I have people in my corner, but I still feel like I am jeopardizing the safety of those I love. I don't know what Dewayne might do if the detectives we have been working with are able to turn up the pressure.

"Hey, how are you doing?" Jason asked. He must have noticed me starting to zone out a bit.

"I'm a little better now actually. I'm glad my parents came." I confess to him.

"I told you, all they want is you to be happy and safe." he says as he starts getting his chair made out into a bed again.

"Jason, you can go home and sleep in a real bed you know." I let tell him. It has been so great having him here, but it can't be comfortable at all. I also worry about how much time he has been away from the bar.

"No chance in hell Kay."

"It's been days now; it can't be easy on you." I tell him. I feel his hand cup my chin as he looks me in the eyes with a look I have never seen on him before, almost one of desire.

"I am never leaving you again" He whispers, and I feel a spark of electricity through my body at his words. What the hell is happening right now? I have never felt that towards Jason before, but he has also never looked at me like this before. I am so confused right now.

After a brief confused pause "Thank you" is the only response I can manage to come up with in the moment and it makes me feel a little silly. I am sure I am misreading the situation and it's making me a little flustered. He finishes making his bed and we get settled in for the night. I will be so happy to finally get out of the hospital, I think it's making me a little crazy.

Chapter 9 Jason

It feels so damn good to finally be home. A couple weeks in a hospital was no fun at all, but I sure as hell wasn't going to leave Kaylee there alone. Maddox did a great job keeping everything up and running at the bar in my absence and the crew really rallied for Kaylee. It will be back to reality for me tomorrow though, but Kaylee will be out for a few more weeks. Thankfully I will be right downstairs if she needs anything and Zane is here for a few more days. She is set up pretty good though. I gave her the bedroom so she can have the bed and Zane and I are taking the living room.

"I think this is the last load of stuff" Zane says as he puts the last couple vases of flowers on the table in the living room.

"Thanks man. I think she got enough flowers and balloons we could start our own shop." I joke with him getting a good laugh. It's shitty circumstances but it is really nice to have him here again. I know Kaylee has enjoyed it too.

I finish helping get the bedroom set up for Kaylee. There is lack of furniture in the place so I fit what vases I can on the dresser, and I leave the rest on the kitchen table for now. At least it adds a little something to the otherwise pretty empty room. I had gone and grabbed what I could out of her place before I went over to the hospital, it wasn't much but she at least has a few sets of clothes and some toiletries for now.

"It looks like all I need for tonight really is something to sleep in." Kaylee says sadly as she looks through the dresser.

"I'm sorry I couldn't grab more. I'll get you some sweatpants and a shirt." I tell her as I wrap my arms around her to offer comfort. It is killing me to see her like this.

"Come on. Let's get you set up in the bathroom. A real shower will do you some good." I say softly

"HAVE YOU TOLD KAYLEE how you feel yet?" Zane questions as I hand him the food that I had the kitchen prepare for him and Kaylee.

"Not yet. I feel like it's still too soon." I say with a heavy sigh. I know I should, but she has been through so much.

"I think you should. Probably sooner rather than later, like before she catches you staring at her with drool running down your chin." He says with a chuckle

"Get the fuck out of here" I laugh.

"Just saying. I've seen it, she might think you're a creep or something." He jokes as he turns to leave

"I'll tell her... Eventually" I holler as he heads up the stairs. He's right, not about the drooling part, but I have been sending some pretty confusing signals lately. I just really don't want to come on too strong. Zane fly's out in the morning so maybe after that I will have some time to talk about it.

As I get done prepping my station for the pending rush I am greeted by Detective Hail form the Harrison Police Department.

"Hey Jason. Do you have a minute?" He asks with a seriousness that puts me a little on edge.

"Uh, Ya. Come on into the office" I tell him trying not to show how unsettled I am starting to feel. After I close the door, he proceeds to tell me about the massive corruption that they have been uncovering, like it's any surprise to me. He informs me that Judge Lavey didn't just cover for Dewayne but some of his friends, as well as county employees. They also compiled a significantly long list of people he was bribing and accepting bribes from. There were large amounts of misuse of county funds, and a pretty long list of inappropriate judgments handed out over some years.

"The plan is to get the feds involved but we don't know if some of the informants will start backing out as this thing moves forward. It's one thing to talk to us but going into a court room face to face can be too much." Detective Hail says.

"So, what does this mean for Kaylee?" I ask unable to hide my concern.

"Well, it means it's probably going to get really ugly as the heat gets cranked up on it. I never would have guessed we would see this much out here in these parts, but the whole county is corrupt over there, be careful." His warning puts knots in my stomach and brings a sense of fear over me. I have no clue how I am going to be able to tell Kaylee about this.

Chapter 10 Kaylee

The news of what is going on in the case has left me rattled. My family and friends are quite possibly in as much danger as I am. I really hope this can all be over soon. I just really don't know what got into Dewayne that night. I was used to getting beat, pretty regularly, but that look in his eye was demonic. He had thrown out all regard for what his dad had warned him about. He was out for blood, and he left me for dead. Could he really have thought he could get away with murder, or did he finally just snap and not care. Either way, he is more dangerous now than ever before.

The sound of my phone ringing pulls me from my thoughts, and I smile a little when I see that it's Jason. He has been so weird lately, but I think I am liking it, maybe a little too much even.

"Hey" I answer trying to not sound like I was just deep in negative thought.

"Hey, I just thought I would check in and see how you're doing." Jason confesses

"I'm fine." I say almost with a smile. He has been so overprotective lately but not in his normal way, it's different somehow.

"Are you hungry? I can have the guys make you food." He offers

"Sounds great, but I'm coming down there today to get it." I say firmly. I am going crazy being stuck in here. I am too scared to venture out, but I am about to lose my shit being shut in.

"Kay, are you sure?" He asks with concern

"Yes, the bruises have faded, and I no longer look like Frankenstein full of stitches. Besides it's karaoke night." I tell him unwilling to let him talk me out of it.

"Then I guess it's settled. I'll see you soon." He can barely get the words out before I hang up. Thank fucking god I have something to do. I head into the bedroom to change into something halfway presentable and try to fix my hair. Moving too much still hurts so I keep my effort minimal and head on downstairs, it's nice I don't have to go far.

My food wasn't ready when I got there but I was greeted with cheers and applause. It felt good to be back in that atmosphere with my friends again, and not hiding a dark secret anymore. After a little bit of mingling, I grabbed my food and headed to the office, I could listen to the signing and talk to my friends, but I didn't have to be around the huge crowd.

Everyone took turns coming in and playing catch up with me. I had a great time listing to all the karaoke, the good and the bad, and I had really missed all the fun bar banter. It was a great night out, and an excellent distraction from all of the Dewayne drama, but it left me so exhausted that I had fallen asleep at the desk while Jason finished closing up. MY slumber was cut short when I feel Jason place his hand on my shoulder.

"Hey, you ready to go home?" he asks softly. When I look up to tell him yes, I am drawn into his gaze. His brown eyes are so captivating, it's like they stare straight into my soul. As I go to stand up, I take the time to actually look at this man, my best friend, who has done everything to not leave my side for weeks. His tan tattooed muscular arms wrap around me so nicely, but I never noticed how built they were. His dark blue jeans and his fitted black tavern shirt show off a perfectly proportioned rock-hard body. How have I never noticed how fucking sexy he is. I feel a familiar jolt run through my body; I felt it in the hospital the first time. I think I am officially turned on by Jason Peterson.

Jason extends his hand toward me so he can escort me back upstairs to the apartment. I gladly accept it and walk beside him. I don't really know what to say right now but my body is feeling sparks, and I am really not sure what to make of it. I continue up the stairs hoping that Jason will say something, anything that might snap me out of this, but nothing. I need to know what is going on here, why has he been so different, is it guilt, is that what he sees when he looks at me? He wanted to get me out of there, he promised he would before something like this happened. I know he tried, does he look at my scares and think he failed? I can't fucking read him, and it is confusing the hell out of me.

"Do you need me to help you with anything?" Jason asked as he walked me into the bedroom.

"Am I broken to you?" I asked unable to control myself I just blurted it out. My tone was almost harsh which was not what I intended

"What do you mean?" Jason asked and his confusion was genuine

"Do you see me as broken Jason? You have been acting so different lately? Am I just some broken thing that you feel responsible for?" I ask with tears pricking at my eyes. I knew when I said it that it was unfair but I have to know.

"God no! Kaylee is that really what you think?" He asks, confusion still wearing on his face and it makes me feel a little bad

"I don't know what I think Jason. You don't hardly leave my side, holding my hand, hugging me with your big sexy biceps, kissing my forehead. It just doesn't feel like the normal big brother thing I am used to from you." I tell him. My tone softer than before but tears still threatening to fall.

"What is it with you and this damn big brother complex bullshit Kaylee. You're my best friend, that's what it was. I never looked at you like a little sister, ever." He says firmly, his voice slightly raised

"I just always thought you did, I'm sorry." I say almost flinching at his firm tone and I can't stop the tears beginning to fall. It makes me feel bad because he noticed and I know he wasn't trying to startle me.

"I'm sorry Kaylee. I shouldn't have said it like that." He says as he says scooping me into his arms. "And I never should have let you believe that's how I saw you." He adds

"Well exactly how do you see me then Jason?" I ask after composing myself and pulling away but only a little "Because I am really confused. It doesn't always seem like just friends either."

"Look, Kaylee, the truth is." He pauses and turns away and it makes me silently whimper a little at the loss of his touch.

"What Jason?" I push for the truth, needing to know now.

"You almost died, and I..I let it happen because I wasn't there for you." He confesses with tears in his eyes. My heart clenches in my chest at the fact he feels responsible, maybe a small part of him does really see me as broken.

"Jason, it's not your fault." I say softly

"It is Kaylee! It is because I didn't fight for you. I should have told you that I..." He trails off as he sits on the bed and hangs his head

"Told me what Jason." I demand, thinking the worst. Did he know Dewayne beat up on women and not tell me?

"I... I'm in love with you Kaylee. For a long time now. I should have told you, before you met Dewayne." He says, full of regret. Silence fills the room for what seems like hours because I am so shocked by his confession. How did I not know, would it have even changed anything? Better yet, how do I process this now that I do know?

"Hey look, I'm sorry I dumped this all on you tonight. It's late so I'll let you get some rest." He says noticing that I am not sure what to say right now. He walks over and gives me a small kiss on the forehead and heads out of the room. He stops at the door and turns to add some comic relief "do you really think my biceps are sexy" as he extends one arm up to show it off.

"Christ Jason" I chuckle as he leaves the room. That was a lot to process and more then what I bargained for when I opened up the conversation. I crawl in bed and let the much-needed sleep consume me.

Chapter 11 Jason

I woke up in the morning with the conversation still heavy on my mind. I feel relieved to finally get my feelings for Kaylee off my chest, but it fucking crushed me to hear that she thought I saw her as broken and only wanted to take care of her because I felt guilty for it. I feel guilty for not doing more but I want to take care of her because I am in love with her. This whole situation it fucked up, her life the last few years has been a prison, it hasn't gotten any better either. She's locked up in here, scared to go anywhere because that asshole is still out there getting away with leaving her for dead.

I start a pot of coffee and get ready for work trying to be as quiet as I can, so I don't wake Kaylee. It's my early day so hopefully tonight we can talk a little more. She just stood there silent after I told her I loved her, I'm not sure how she is taking that information. I just hope she feels kind of the same way. I really don't want to rush her right now, Dewayne did a lot of fucked up shit to her, but it would be nice if she thought that we could be something. I down a cup of coffee and prep another one to take with me. Before heading down to the bar, I make sure to leave Kaylee a note.

Just have some deliveries and inventory to deal with today. I'll be home in a few hours. Hope we can talk later.

I FINALLY FINISH UP putting the deliveries away and inputting all the inventory when I realize it's almost 5. I decided to have the guys start making me something to take home for me and Kaylee before I find Maddox.

"Hey Maddox. I'm taking off but everything is put away and accounted for. If you guys run into any issues, call me." I tell him as I head to the door.

"No problem, we'll see you tomorrow." he says as I make my exit

When I get home, I am surprised that I don't see Kaylee anywhere.

"Kaylee, I'm home" I call out to her "I brought food"

As I get the food laid out on the table, I hear the bathroom door open, so I turn around. I see Kaylee walk out in nothing but her towel and her ear pods. I can't help but stare at her, filled with lust. Maybe Zane was a little bit right about the drooling, she is so damn gorgeous.

"Kaylee" I say with a bit of a raised voice.

"Holy shit, Jason. You scared me" she yells as she jumps back a little causing her to almost lose the towel.

"I'm sorry, I didn't mean to startle you. I thought you would have heard me." I say with a deep chuckle, and slightly disappointed the towel was still on "hungry?"

"Uh, ya, let me just go put theses away and get dressed" she says with a smile but still trying to calm her racing heart

"Need any help?" I ask lustfully without thinking. I try to cover by acting playful, she just giggled and walked into the bedroom for a few minutes.

"Jason" I hear Kaylee call out.

When I get to the door I see she is still in her towel. She is so fucking beautiful. Her sun kissed skin looks so soft. Her brown eyes sparkle a little as they reflect the light. Her lips look so inviting as she nervously bites on her bottom one. My dick twitches in my pants a little at the sight of her, I want nothing more than to rip that towel right off of her and reveal what I am sure are her perfect breasts.

"Um.. could you put lotion on my back." She asks nervously. I can't help but smile as I see a blush creep up in her cheeks as I get closer. My guess is she really doesn't need any lotion, and that is just fine with me.

"Turn around" I whisper in her ear as I reach for the lotion bottle. I gently move her long damp brunette hair out of the way. A small quiet gasp escapes her lips as my fingertips brush along her skin. As I gently massage the lotion onto her back, she slowly starts leaning into me. I gently run my hand down her arm and place it around her waist. Her breathing starts to quicken, and I can tell she is becoming aroused at my touch. I still want to take things slow, at her pace.

"Is this ok" I ask in a whisper before sucking her earlobe gently into my mouth.

"Yes" she breathes out softly

I plant soft open mouth kisses down to her neck and slowly place my hand on her upper thigh just at the hem of the towel. I can hear her breath hitch in her throat as I start to slowly and gently caress her inner thigh.

"More" she softly moans out. I slowly bring my hand up and cup her chin so I can gain access to her beautiful lips, crashing mine against hers for our first, deep, passionate kiss. My body temperature rises and my rock-hard dick is aching to get out of my jeans. She breaks the kiss long enough to say "please". I hoist her up; her legs wrap around my hips so I can carry her to the bed.

"Are you sure?" I asks her softly as I lay her gently on the bed. She nods her head before crashing her lips back into mine. I slowly make my way down to the crock of her neck as my hand softly finds her breast. Her nipple is hardened so I softly caress it with the pad of my thumb while my mouth takes its time traveling lower. She moans out in pleasure as I suck her nipple into my mouth. I want to fuck her so bad, but she deserves only passion right now.

Making my way slowly down her curves to her hot, wet, aching center, soft moans escape her lips as she runs her fingers through my hair and pulls my head in closer to her dripping folds. I take a long slow lick before sucking her clit into my mouth. She cries out a pleasure filled "More", and I am all too happy to oblige. Her wish is my every command right now. I gently slide two fingers in her heated folds and start pumping slowly. I love the sounds of her moaning in pleasure. I slowly start pumping faster and allowing my tongue to pick up the pace. I can feel her pussy start to clench a little and her breathing quickens.

Her hands grip my sheets and her toes curl; I feel her pussy start to spasm as her release pours out. Her body shakes as she screams out my name. I am filled with pride at the amount of pleasure I just gave her, but my urge to fuck her is getting stronger, I am so turned on. I crawl up between her legs and give her another deep passionate kiss. Her hands travel toward the button of my jeans, my hard cock ready to burst out, her touch is like electricity sending sparks through my body. I deepen the kiss as I feel her hand tug at my now unbuttoned jeans. I am so ready to take her but only at her ask.

"I want you, Jason." She softly whispered. That was all I needed to hear, and I was ready. I finished taking of my pants and I lined my hard cock up at her still dripping center. I eased it in slow, but I couldn't help but moan out. She feels so fucking good. I keep my pace slow and steady at first, I wait for her moans and her words to guide me. Soon a lust filled "faster" escapes her lips. At her command I piston my hips faster, I place the pad of my thumb on her hardened nub. I can tell she is being sent over the edge because I can feel her walls starting to spasm on my thrusting cock. Uncontrollable pleasure filled moans fall from her, I ride her release out all the way to mine filling her walls fully. Collapsing on the bed next to her, I pull her naked body in against mine.

Chapter 12 Kaylee

I couldn't help myself any longer. I wanted him, no needed him, all of him. I was so nervous, but I had to come up with an excuse for him to touch me. I needed to know that he meant what he said last night. He was so gentle, so attentive, so loving. It was different than anything I have felt in years. I can't believe that I didn't see it, for years I missed it. Jason was in love with me, and I never knew it. I was pretty harsh in my words to him when I got with Dewayne, I really thought he was just being extra overprotective because Zane wasn't around much. I shrugged off his warning in the worst way and then he had to watch as I became more and more trapped in a toxic hell that I couldn't ever manage to escape.

I could lay right here in his arms forever right now; I feel so comfortable and safe. My body molds perfectly to his broad chest and defined abdomen. His large biceps feel amazing wrapped around my small frame, and the smell of his cologne is intoxicating. I frown a little when I hear the ping of his phone, I don't want this to end. I softly whimper at the loss of his touch as he checks his phone.

"Hey love. It was Maddox. He says it's urgent!" I'll be back up as soon as I can" he says softly before giving me a deep passionate kiss.

"See you soon" I say softly as my heart clenches in my chest a little bit at the thought of being apart. I miss him already and he hasn't even left yet.

"HOW THE FUCK AM I SUPPOSED to calm down Jason!" I scream as the results of the urgent message that Maddox sent are ringing in my ear. Fucking vandalizing property to try to bully people into staying quiet, including my parents, that fucking sounds like something Dewayne would do.

"What if he gets away with this shit!" I cry unable to stop the tears from falling like rain.

"They're going to catch him, Kay. Vandalizing cars and homes take time, they are onto him, it's only a matter of time before he is caught in the act. Judge Lavey is on leave because of the investigation, Detective Hail is confident it will all stick even with all of this." He tries to comfort me with that statement but all I can think about is the growing number of people who are no longer willing to come forward against all the shady ass shit happening in Hamilton County. I'm sure on paper they have enough to put Judge Lavey in prison, but he's not even in handcuffs yet. Dewayne is a different story all together, other than the ass kicking he just gave me there really isn't much documented, and suspicious vandalism doesn't exactly scream federal case.

"I just want it to be over Jason" I whisper as I cling to him as if my life were dependent on it.

"They're going to get him love." He says softly as he gently kisses my forehead. I hope he's right; I want to move on, I need to move on.

Chapter 13 Kaylee

"Are you sure your ready love, you really don't have to go back yet." Jason asks me with genuine concern warring on his face.

"I have to Jason. I really need it." I plea with him. It is, after all, still his bar, and he is still my boss. I am nervous of the newly developing dynamic between us because I'm not exactly sure where we stand yet, but I have to get back to work.

"Ok love" I damn near melt every time I hear his new name for me roll off of his tongue. "But I don't want you to overdo it." He adds before cupping my chin in his hand and giving me a soft kiss.

"I won't. I'll see you down there."

I PROMISED JASON THAT I would take it easy for the first few days back, so I pretty much stayed at the counter and mixed drinks all night. I felt a little rusty after being gone for several weeks but I thought it went good for my first night back. It was definitely a welcomed distraction from all of the drama and confusion over the last few days. It seemed to go alright working side by side with Jason but there was definitely some sexual tension, on my part at least. Even in this bar I could smell the amazing woodsy musk of his cologne. I loved the way his dark gray t-shirt hugged his biceps exposing his tattooed muscular form. I was mesmerized at the way his dark blue relaxed fit jeans flawlessly sat around his perfect ass. I couldn't stop myself from getting distracted by thoughts of taking them off of him.

I finished up all of my closing duties and met Jason in the office. We haven't talked much about what happened the other day, but I am not really in the mood for much talking at all. I need to have him again; I need to feel him. Right now, I am ready to show him what I'm feeling rather than taking about it. With my eyes full of lust and an ache at my core I close the door behind me even though I am sure we are alone. I walk up and wedge myself between him and the desk so I can straddle him. I see surprise and desire rise in his face. He parts his lips to start to speak but like I said, I'm not in the mood for talking. I crash my lips into his before any words can be spoken, instead all I hear is a deep lustful groan. His hands find their way to my ass pulling me in closer to him, I feel the arousal rise in his jeans and my lips curl into a smile against his.

My hands find the bottom of his shirt so I can remove it revealing his broad chest and tight, lean stomach. I plant small open mouth kisses on his neck as I trail my fingertips over his defined muscles moving them slowly toward his jeans. Low moans full of desire escape his lips as I unbutton his jeans and free his hard cock. I wrap my hand around his girth as I suck his earlobe into my mouth, his breathing quickens in response. I beg a breathy "please" in his ear, I am so damn eager to feel him, taste him. A deep lust filled growl rumbles in his chest at my words, and it sends a wave of heat to my already burning core.

I run my mouth down his body leaving a trail of open mouth kisses as I slowly slide to my knees. I take a hard slow lick up his large shaft, teasing him, before wrapping my lips around it sucking it into my mouth. I feel his hand gently wrap up in my long hair, holding it out of the way as he moans out in pleasure. I keep my pace slow at first, taking my time, savoring his taste as my tongue dances along his perfect cock. I move my mouth up and down keeping my suction steady as I start to move faster. I want so desperately for him to cum, he makes me want to please him, to satisfy him. Deep, loud cries of pleasure come as he finds his release.

Looking up at him through my lashes I grin as I see the completely sated look on his face. A combination of pride and arousal take over as it sinks in that I did that to him; I made him feel that way. I prop myself up against the desk after standing, I still can't help but stare at Jason with complete desire. I think I have fallen madly in love with this man.

"Take me home baby" I say softly extending my hand out for his.

Chapter 14 Jason

I was pleasantly caught off guard by Kaylee last night. We had slept together a few days ago but Detective Hail's visit soon after with an update in the case really kind of overshadowed the amazing moment we shared. Kaylee and I hadn't really had a chance to talk about what had happened or what it even meant for us. I wasn't really sure what to think or to expect when she came into the office and closed the door, it wasn't like her. I wasn't going to ask any fucking questions though when she sat down and crashed her perfectly plump lips against mine. The way her eyes filled with lust when she begged me "please" had my dick so fucking hard for her. The pleasure was so intense, and it left me wanting to do the same for her.

By the time we got home I could hardly stand it, I had to get her naked. I pinned her against the door and crashed my lips into hers. She parted my lips with her tongue deepening the kiss. Grabbing at her shirt I lift it up over her head revealing her beautiful tender breasts. A gasp fell from her lips as I sucked her nipple into my mouth, she moaned out in pleasure as I took my time gently devouring it. Hoisting her up around my hips by her ass I carried her to the bedroom, she lets out a small sequel as we fell to the bed. I kissed at her collarbone and inched my way toward her waist. I teased her a little running my fingertips along the top of her jeans before slowly removing them.

My dick jumped in my pants at the sight of her purple lace panties. She moaned out a breathy "more" as I kissed her hips making my way toward her heated center. Her screams of ecstasy sounded so sweet as I sucked her clit into my mouth. I slid my two fingers inside her dripping folds curving them slightly, her toes started to curl, and her moans got louder as I pumped my fingers faster. Her pussy clenched around my fingers as she found her release. I held her close as she laid there breathless.

"Sleep here with me." She whispered as she drifted off to sleep. There was no way I was going to say no to that. It was a perfect night followed by a perfect morning. I woke up this morning to Kaylee's naked body still wrapped comfortably in my arms. I want this every day, waking up next to my best friend and the most beautiful girl in the world, it doesn't get much better. I decide to sneak away long enough to brew a pot of coffee and make a couple bagels for us.

"Good morning love" I whisper softly as I set the coffee and bagels down on the nightstand.

"Good morning" she responds through a yawn

"I brought you a cup of coffee and a bagel"

"Thank you. I'm starting to feel a little spoiled" She jokes

"I wouldn't have it any other way" I chuckle back as I walk to the dresser to grab her a t-shirt.

"It felt good being back to work. I really missed it"

"I'm glad. You looked like you were having a good time." I tell her as I hand her the t-shirt.

"I had a great time. I am glad I went back on a weekday though because I was a little rusty." She giggles as she puts on her shirt. "I also kept getting distracted." she adds

"Oh ya. By what?" I ask with my brow lifted in curiosity

"There was this really good-looking bartender next to me with a great smile and sexy biceps." She flirted, making a chuckle rise from deep in my chest.

"Sounds like I might need to have a talk with this good-looking bartender of yours and tell him to go away." I tease as I inch closer to her

"You probably should, he's very distracting." She says playfully

"I'll tell him your mine love." I tell her as I lean into her, and I notice a blush rise to her cheeks.

"I like the sound of that" She whispers before placing her soft lips on mine. God, I love it when she kisses me.

Chapter 15 Kaylee

"You can do this Kay" I tell myself as I look in the mirror at the scars that have been left on my body. The everyday reminder of the hell that I was trapped in for years, a hell that almost cost me my life. Today I am supposed to face the monster who left them, the ruler of my hell. Today I will sit on the stand at Dewayne's trial and look him in the eye while I tell my story. I have been trying to put it all behind me for months now but today I will have to relive every detail. The prosecution will ask me about the abuse that I endured over the years but focusing heavily on the night I want to forget the most, the night Dewayne left me for dead. They will want me to walk them through the escalation over the years from the first hit to the very last one that left me fading into the darkness as I laid there on my kitchen floor. The defense will try to paint a much different picture of him though; they will try to place attention on how he was in the beginning. The sweet, charming man that showered me with gifts, the man I fell in love with. They will call into question my judgment for not leaving him. They will try to place their focus on the fact that I stopped reporting it.

I pray that I can be strong enough for this, that I won't completely break down on the stand. I have not seen Dewayne in months and even though he is in finally behind bars now there is still a part of me that is terrified of him. My freedom from him and my justice depends on my strength to testify today. I really need the closure. I was finally able to breathe a little easier when we got the call from Detective Hail that Dewayne had finally been arrested, but I want a conviction. I want to know that the fucking prick will be locked up for many years to come. I just want to feel safe again. I want to feel free again. I want to be able to build my life with Jason without detectives, lawyers and court dates.

"You are going to do just fine love" Jason whispers as he zips up the zipper of my dress I was struggling with through my nervousness.

"I'm getting scared. What if I can't face him and this fails?" I say as tears threaten to prick my eyes

"He's not walking this time Kay, he's not. You are so strong, you can do this." He reassures me. I take a deep breath and offer a smile in return. Jason always knows what I need to hear, he is my rock and my savior, I don't think I will ever be able to thank him enough for it.

"I love you Jason Peterson" I say softly as I nestle my head in his chest for comfort

"I love you too Kaylee Thomas." He says as he wraps his arms around me and kisses my forehead. "Now let's go"

My time on the stand seemed like it took hours, and it was painful to see the pictures that the detectives took while I was in the hospital. Dewayne's reaction to my account of that night was cold and uncaring. He even chuckled a little as I painfully described being dragged down the stairs. By the time the trial was over the defense team had done a pretty poor job of making him out to be anything other than the monster that he is. There was some pretty damning evidence presented though.

Tears of joy and relief fell uncontrollably down my face when the words, "We find the defendant Dewayne Lavey guilty on the charge of attempted murder", were said out loud. A year ago, I thought I was going to be stuck in that hell forever. I thought my only way out was going to be when Dewayne killed me and he almost did. My story didn't end that night though, thanks to Jason and the nice couple who lived next door who just finally got fed up, my story gets to go on. Dewayne's chapter is closed for good, and my happily ever after with Jason is just beginning.

Thank you for reading!

Please write a review.

Don't miss out!

Visit the website below and you can sign up to receive emails whenever Melissa C publishes a new book. There's no charge and no obligation.

https://books2read.com/r/B-A-MKNCB-SIDAE

BOOKS 2 READ

Connecting independent readers to independent writers.

MELISSA C
Addicted
To You

Also by Melissa C

Liquor and Lust
Addicted To You
Save Me

Watch for more at https://x.com/melissaC589024.

About the Author

I have always enjoyed writing steamy stories, but I have always viewed them as silly. I have always just deleted my work instead of finishing it, let alone publishing it. I finaly decided "What the heck, I love it so why not work on it" I enjoy the freedom self publishing brings me. I can write around my job, my kids, and our homestead. Between my full time job in caregiving, my 6 homeschooled children and all the chores, writing is my peace, my me time. I hope that my stories can bring entertainment to my readers because it brings me so much joy to write them.

Read more at https://x.com/melissaC589024.

About the Publisher

I love being an author and publisher all in one. I love the freedom of creating all my own material at my own pace.

www.ingramcontent.com/pod-product-compliance
Lightning Source LLC
Chambersburg PA
CBHW021352160726
47994CB00007B/2933